D0021317

A NOTE TO PARENTS

Disney's **First Readers Level 1** books were developed with the beginning reader in mind. They feature large, easy-to-read type, lots of repetition, and simple vocabulary.

One of the most important ways parents can help their child develop a love of reading is by providing an *environment* of reading. Every time you discuss a book, read aloud to your child, or your child observes you reading, you promote the development of early reading skills and habits. Here are some tips to help you use **Disney's First Readers Level 1** books with your child:

★ Tell the story about the original Disney film or video. Storytelling is crucial to language development. A young child needs a language *foundation* before reading skills can begin to emerge.

★ Talk about the illustrations in the book. Beginning readers need to use illustrations to gather clues about unknown words or to understand the story.

★ Read aloud to your child. When you read aloud, smoothly run your finger under the text. Do not stop at each word. Enliven the text for your child by using a different voice for each character. In other words, be an actor—and have fun!

★ "Read it again!" Children love hearing stories read again and again. When they begin reading on their own, repetition helps them feel successful. Maintain patience, be encouraging, and expect to read the same books over and over.

★ Play "question and answer." Use the After-Reading Fun activities provided at the end of each book to further enhance your child's learning process.

Remember that early-reading experiences that you share with your child can help him or her to become a confident and successful reader later on!

— Patricia Koppman
Past President
International Reading Association

Pencils by Karen Rosenfield, Denise Shimabukuro, Orlando De La Paz

First published by Disney Press, New York, New York.
This edition published by Scholastic Inc.,
90 Old Sherman Turnpike, Danbury, Connecticut 06816
by arrangement with Disney Licensed Publishing.

SCHOLASTIC and associated logos are trademarks of Scholastic Inc.

ISBN 0-7172-8885-4

Printed in the U.S.A.

ROAR!

by Patricia Grossman
Illustrated by Adam Devaney
and Darren Hont

Disney's First Readers — Level 1
A Story from Disney's *The Lion King*

SCHOLASTIC INC.

New York Toronto London Auckland Sydney
Mexico City New Delhi Hong Kong Buenos Aires

The day begins.
Simba and Nala
start to roar.

Simba roars at all the
tall giraffes.

They just toss their heads.

Nala roars at the
busy monkeys.

They just laugh.

Simba roars
at the big
elephants.

They just trumpet back.

Nala roars at the young zebras.

They just keep eating.

Then
Simba
and Nala
see Zazu.

Zazu is napping
high in a tree.

Simba roars at Zazu.

Zazu just keeps napping.

Nala roars at Zazu.

Zazu just keeps dreaming.

Simba roars *again* at Zazu.

Zazu just keeps snoring.

At last,
Simba and
Nala *both*
roar at Zazu.

Good-bye, nap.
Good-bye, dreams.
Good-bye, snores.

"Go roar somewhere
else!" shouts Zazu.

Enhance the reading experience with follow-up questions to help your child develop reading comprehension and increase his/her awareness of words.

Approach this with a sense of play. Make a game of having your child answer the questions. You do not need to ask all the questions at one time. Let these questions be fun discussions rather than a test. If your child doesn't have instant recall, encourage him/her to look back into the book to "research" the answers. You'll be modeling what good readers do and, at the same time, forging a sharing bond with your child.

1. Name all the animals that Simba roars at.

2. What do the zebras do when Nala roars at them?

3. Why do you think Zazu naps in a tree?

4. Name all the things Simba and Nala can see around them.

5. What words in the story end with the letters -ing?

6. How many words can you think of that start like "<u>dr</u>eam"?

Answers: 1. giraffes, elephants, Zazu. **2.** they just keep eating. **3.** *possible answers:* it's Zazu's home. it's a safe place to sleep. **4.** *possible answers:* plants, trees, grass, rocks, sky, other animals. **5.** eating, napping, dreaming, snoring. **6.** *possible answers:* dry, drum, drink, drip, drop, draw.